Not Quite Cinderella

LIANA BROOKS

OTHER WORKS

HEROES AND VILLAINS

Even Villains Fall In Love
Even Villains Go To The Movies
Even Villains Have Interns
Even Villains Play The Hero (books 1 – 3 omnibus)
The Polar Terror

FLEET OF MALIK

Bodies In Motion
Change of Momentum
For Every Action (forthcoming)

SHORTER WORKS

All I Want For Christmas Is A Werewolf
Fey Lights
Prime Sensations
Darkness and Good

Find other works by the author at
www.lianabrooks.com

Not Quite Cinderella

INKLET #40

AMY LAURENS

Inkprint
PRESS
www.inkprintpress.com

Print ISBN: 978-1-925825-39-8
eBook ISBN: 9781393673316

www.inkprintpress.com

National Library of Australia Cataloguing-in-Publication Data
Brooks, Liana 1982 –
Not Quite Cinderella
48 p.
ISBN: 978-1-925825-39-8
Inkprint Press, Canberra, Australia
1. Fiction—Fantasy—General 2. Fiction—Fairy Tales, Folk Tales, Legends & Mythology 3. Fiction—Short Stories

First Print Edition: August 2020
Cover image © Ingeborg Grein via Unsplash
Cover design © Inkprint Press
Interior art © Amy Laurens

NOT QUITE CINDERELLA

"HAVE YOU HEARD? THE PRINCE IS giving a ball!"

"In the middle of a war?" Marian looked at the thin, sallow pastry chef behind the counter who didn't look like he'd ever tasted his own wares. "Are you serious? A party during a major offensive?"

The sallow chef nodded eagerly. "Oh, yes! The prince will choose a bride, the king will abdicate, and the whole war will be over."

Marian nodded slowly, weighing the options. "So, what I'm hearing is, your side is losing?"

"My side?" The thin man looked confused.

"The king is losing, isn't he?"

The man's eyes widened. "I would never suggest something so traitorous!"

"Of course not." She gave him a polite smile. "One fudge brownie, please." She pointed to the rich confection and waited as he bagged her purchase. Her sponsors couldn't afford for the war to end now.

"Three coppers."

She slid a silver piece across the counter. "The stars shine on those who show charity today," she said and walked out with the brownie, skirts swirling around her. An end to the war. Not good. Still, it could be fixed easily enough. Plans began to circulate through her mind.

The baker wasn't the only one with news of the ball. In the centre of town the square buzzed with people rushing to prepare for the upcoming party. Dress shops, barely open for the day, had lines of customers and coaches waiting outside. The grocer's cart was empty. Flower sellers were scarce, or possibly just waiting in line for a seasonable dress.

One very determined hat seller stepped into Marian's path, advancing at her with a bright green horror stuffed with purple feathers. "Have you something fetching to wear to the ball, Mi'lady?"

"No," Marian said, trying to sidestep the feather tickling her nose.

"Have you considered green, Mi' lady? It would be a most becoming color on you."

"Yes, if I had darker skin or fairer hair I'm sure it would. But since I have neither, I think perhaps not." She offered the hat seller a strained smile.

"Purple?" The hat seller waved the plumes closer to her face.

"No, lime and plum aren't the right shades for me," she said. *Or anyone with a modicum of taste.* "Thank you."

The hat seller pounced, placing the hat on her head and stabbing it in place with a five-inch hairpin.

Marian glared as she counted, in Greek, to ten. "Remove the hat."

"But for just a few silvers..." the seller wheedled.

"*REMOVE THE HAT.*" Thunder cracked through the clear sky.

The seller grabbed the hat, ripping the felt, and ran.

Marian removed the pin from her hair and tossed it on the ground. Around her, the natives edged away, fearful of what she might do next.

She rolled her eyes and walked back to the inn she'd checked into late last night.

It wasn't the fanciest place she'd ever spent the night, but it certainly wasn't the worst.

She tossed a small bag of silver pieces to the innkeeper for a hot bath and a warm meal, and walked up the stairs, musing over the worst place she'd spent the night. Probably in the burnt-out hovel last year, where the ruins were still smoking and the air smelled of burnt flesh. She'd slept on the floor in the stone cellar, waiting for the pain to stop.

Opening the door to her small room, Marian paused. No, the cellar was the second worst. The first worst had to have been that palace three years back, with the hideous pink silk and white lace covering everything. That was the worst. Definitely.

Someone appeared behind her. "Water, Miss, for your bath, Miss."

She turned and smiled at the fresh-faced maid carrying two buckets of steaming water. "Please, bring them in."

"Here you go, miss. Getting ready for the ball, are you?"

"Me?" Marian shook her head. "I wasn't planning to."

The girl sighed, starry eyed. "Oh, but a ball. Doesn't everyone want to go and dance the night away?"

Marian wrinkled her nose. "Pinched shoes, creaking corsets, and the smell of old women marinating in their perfume? It really isn't that grand."

"But to meet the prince!" The girl put the buckets by the fireplace, not spilling a drop. "I'd love to go, just for that." She didn't swoon, but she did sigh.

Meet the prince, yes. "And I suppose your wicked stepmother is making you stay home and polish the silver?"

The girl blushed. "No, Mother wouldn't mind if I went. But I've nothing to wear. Nothing nice. I wouldn't get past the guards."

Marian debated for a moment, and decided she was feeling generous. She waved her hand. "Nonsense! You're quite a lovely girl. Hurry and draw my bath and perhaps I can find a suitable tip for you."

The girl curtsied. "That's quite all right, Miss. Even if we had a spare silver or two, all the nice dresses have been bought up by now."

Marian shooed her out. "Get my bath and let me worry about the tip."

She opened the door to the room's armoire and studied the dresses inside. Fine blonde hair, pink cheeks, deep blue eyes and brown, muddy feet...

The girl needed something full length, soft and dusky. Marian discarded red immediately: too wanton. And pink was abjectly cruel: the poor girl would look like a shepherdess who'd lost her nursery rhyme. Blue was the obvious answer, but was it too obvious? Yes, yes it was. She could do better.

From the back of the armoire, she pulled out a lilac gown of silk, with seed pearls and diamonds fastened around the low collar. Perfect. Even if the girl didn't net the prince in this affair (which might be a blessing considering the political situation), she'd find some suitor willing to marry her for the dress alone.

The maid backed into the room, carrying the wooden sitting tub, red and shiny in the face.

"Just set it down there by the fireplace," Marian instructed. "I know it's too warm for a fire, but it does seem the proper place for a bath. Do you have a screen, perchance?" She waved at the view. "The windows are lovely but, well, a maiden and her modesty and all that..."

The maid turned around, nodding again, and stopped to stare at the gown. "Oh! That's the most beautiful thing I've ever seen! Did you change your mind? Are you going tonight after all?"

"Hmm. I may. But this old thing?" Marian made a show of regarding the gown with great skepticism. "It really isn't my color. Far too regal, and too pale for my skin, I think. Do you like it?"

The maid wiped her hands on her own brown skirt before gently running the hem of the lilac gown through her fingers. "It's lovely."

"I really do think it's a tattered old thing. You can have it if you like." Marian tossed the dress at her. "Go and try it on. If you hurry, your mother will have time to fit it to you before the ball."

Her eyes went wide. "But, your bath..."

Marian shrugged. "I can handle that. Go on, have fun tonight." The maid left hurriedly. Marian hummed to herself. She bathed, ate a leisurely meal while watching people bustle through the streets in preparation for the festival, and then took a nap.

She woke when the bell tower tolled ten. With practiced moves, she dressed in a pristine white gown with a belled skirt and a low neckline. A white opal pendant that flashed fire in the candlelight completed the ensemble. In the window she could see her reflection, a perfect vision of a mysterious princess arriving late for the ball. Down in the alley she could even see the perfect coach, just waiting to whisk her away.

How banal.

Marian swept down the stairs and out the back door, unnoticed by the snoozing innkeeper. The coachman didn't say a word as she touched her necklace and tucked her head like a coy ingénue. She smiled to herself as they clattered through the cobblestone streets. Charms were almost cheating. Well, not charms plural, Marian reminded herself; charm, singular, and not the kind that witches and sorceresses used. A single, simple charm to make everyone love her.

There was a momentary twinge of guilt. What if the nice little maid had charmed the prince naturally? Marian furrowed her brow, wondering how she would work that one out. As the coach rolled to a stop at the palace gates and the page ran to open the door, the tower bells chimed eleven. With a sigh, Marian gave up the dilemma. All she could do was hope for the best, and kill anyone who got in her way.

With infinite grace, she swept up the stairs and through the halls, pausing to time her entrance with the final flourish in the music for max-imum drama.

The prince's hand dropped away from the waist of the blue-clad beauty he'd been dancing with. Marian curtsied at a distance, hiding a snicker. A pale blue dress on a blue-eyed blonde, with upswept hair? Really? How clichéd could a fairy godmother get? If she had a copper for every time a well-meaning interloper put a blue dress on a blue-eyed girl, she'd have enough for a retirement fund, or at least a vacation somewhere tropical.

She forced a blush as the prince practically ran up the short staircase to bow low over her hand. "May I have this dance?"

"I'd be delighted," she simpered. It took practice to simper, and it paid off. The prince danced her around the room, staring deeply into her eyes like a fool in love.

Later, he took her into the moonlit

gardens. "Am I really in love? Or is this some magic? A dream?" he whispered as he leaned close.

"Magic," Marian whispered too. "Charm enchantment."

"Do you love me?" The prince tenderly brushed a finger along her cheek. "I love you."

"I know." She stepped away from him. "But it won't last past dawn."

He stepped closer. "If we have only to dawn, let us dance the night away."

"Virgin!" She smothered a laugh in her hand, pretending to cough. Recovering herself, she smiled at the prince. "I have a carriage. Let's run away together."

He put his hands on her hips and pulled her close. "I'll do anything you say."

"Smart kid." Marian patted his cheek. "Take my hand and lead me the back way to the carriages. And then pick the fastest one."

"Where are we going?" he asked, showing the first real sign of independent thought. A strong-willed person would fight the charm enchantment; the prince wasn't fighting at all. Really, she was doing the kingdom a favor by removing him from the line for the throne. "My love?"

"We're running away together," Marian told him as he led her through dark rose gardens and down marble steps to the courtyard full of carriages. The rub of her knife sheath as she descended the stairs was a comforting caress. "By the way, you have a beautiful castle."

"We have a beautiful castle," he told her. "Forever we, you and I together in love."

"At least until death or dawn do us part." Marian let him hand her into the carriage. In a high up window she saw a young woman, radiant in lilac and diamonds, flirting with a powerful

young duke. At least someone would
have a happy ending.

THE MAKING OF
NOT QUITE CINDERELLA

I'm not the kind of person who can be trusted to watch period movies. Cinderella, in all its many variants, has always perplexed me. What kind of person decides they want to run a kingdom with a person they met at a dance? Wouldn't you at least want to run a background check to make sure they weren't a spy?

These little thoughts start stories, and possibly wars.

DOWNLOAD YOUR FREE EBOOK

When you buy a print book from Inkprint Press, we like to say THANK YOU by offering you the ebook for free!

Please head to www.inkprintpress.com/inklets/40/ and the use the coupon 40INK to get your copy of this Inklet in epub AND mobi today!
(Coupon will only work once.)

Read more by Liana Brooks!

FLEET OF MALIK
BODIES IN MOTION
CHAPTER ONE

THE PROBLEM WITH VACATIONS, Selena reflected as she adjusted her sweater outside Cargo Blue, was that reality was always waiting at the end. A quick search of the local security cameras found one that showed the peeling sunburn on her right shoulder blade.

Such was the curse of pale-skinned, ship-born Fleet personnel. Anytime she left the foggy belts covering the city of Tarrin, she barbecued like a shrimp, no matter how much sunscreen she applied. Otherwise, she'd flee even further from the Fleet Enclave and make her home on the equatorial beaches of the planet they were trapped on.

She panned the camera and checked her left shoulder. Black ink made a star-scape that disguised three silver scars as shooting stars. The painting covered her shoulder blade and part of her upper arm.

As the artist had promised, the skin-paint had kept her from burning as much, though it still had the over-stretched feel of a burn. With a few adjustments, her uniform covered most of the temporary art; it would keep her from having to explain to her colleagues.

Her forearm warmed, a warning that someone was about to contact her through the tech implant tucked between her radius and ulna.

She hesitated too long and the call came through, a persistent ping against her skull as the phantom image of her best friend floated on the edge of her vision.

Selena turned off the visual receiver and answered. "Genevieve," she said with a smile as the image of her vivacious, red-headed friend appeared floating against the backdrop of landing gear that supported the grounded fleet.

A grounder would have thought she was talking to herself, but grounders wouldn't set foot near the neo-city-state of Enclave. The rocky beach served as a city and tomb for the survivors of the last war.

"Selena!" Gen gushed. "Starcom to Selena. Where are you? I'm covering for now."

"Delayed, but almost there." Selena hoped Gen wouldn't hear the lie. She'd been standing in the shadows of the Enclave pub for nearly a quarter hour.

"The *Lorenza* could get here faster," Gen said, referencing a long-dead ship whose crew were found skeletonized at their stations. Gen blew hair off her face. "Stars above, you're an hour late. The whole fleet is flying faster than you."

Selena turned on her visual long enough to roll her eyes at her friend. "Ha, ha, funny. That joke needs to be forcibly retired." Sooner rather than later. The fleet couldn't fly without fuel, and the Malik system they were stranded in held precious few deposits of the orun crystals needed to power the ships.

"If you don't come," Gen said threateningly, "I will teleport to your apartment and drag you out in your pajamas."

"I'm not at home," Selena admitted. And she wouldn't have let her best friend come to her new house if she was.

Gen was smart enough to realize that the small palace Selena had bought in downtown Tarrin wasn't paid for by her official OIA salary. The paygrades for the Office of Imperial Affairs had last been updated when the Malik system was still in contact with the empire, making them 900 years out of date.

Technically, taking a second job wasn't treason, but there were enough people in the fleet who'd see it as a betrayal that keeping it secret felt right. Especially since Gen's captain was one who would scream the loudest.

Gen clapped. "Selena! Stop stalling yer engines and get in here. This isn't some Fleet Tribunal, just our friends. You, me, Carver. I left a message for Marshall. You know. People we like."

The light of understanding dawned. "Carver? This is so you can snuggle up to Perrin Carver without your parents watching?"

"Yes," Gen admitted, not looking the least bit contrite.

"You're only dragging me along so I can cover for you while you make out in a corner, aren't you?" She masked the relief with mock anger. At least Gen wasn't trying to set Selena up with one of her cousins. Or, ancestors forbid, Gen's handsy older brother.

Again.

Gen opened her eyes wide with an innocent smile. "Maybe."

"Gen!" Selena rolled her eyes. "Doesn't he have his own place?"

"Just the bachelor's dorm. The Carvers didn't have any ships except the shuttle his parents crashed in. Making out next door to Mom and Dad? No. And the BOQ? It's so tacky. You can hear everything through those walls."

Selena hid a smile. "I'll be there soon enough."

If Gen ever caught wind of how panicky the thought of a relationship made her, Gen would make it her life's goal to see Selena paired off. And there wasn't a man alive who she could imagine getting close to now.

Her implant helpfully pulled up an image of a tall, broad-shouldered, lean-muscled fighter with skin black as the night between stars and emerald-green eyes.

She pushed the memory away.

Lieutenant Commander Titan Sciarra was striking, intelligent, and had a body she'd cross battle lines for, but he was also out of reach. There was no point in chasing a man who wouldn't give her the time of day.

Another crew shuffled past her into the bar, black patches with silver fists on their shoulders.

It was getting harder to pretend she belonged in Enclave, with the fleet. Once upon a time, she'd known every crew's patch without thinking. She could name captains, their ships and their seconds by rote.

Now she would need to tap into the fleet's information nexus if she wanted to know who they were.

She stopped at the edge of the door to tug her lightest shields into place. A few minor adjustments would keep bugs away, keep beer off her clothes, and prevent anyone from hacking into her implant. They could still send messages, because disallowing that would have raised eyebrows. And they could still hit her. But she could always hit back.

Selena rolled her shoulders and strutted into Cargo Blue. It was a battle-field, but she was the last captain of the Caryll family, and she wasn't going down without a fight.

Whatever crew owned Cargo Blue probably hadn't had much of a decorating budget, but at least they'd stuck with a theme: oversized cargo boxes were piled up to make walls, seating, and tables. Olive-green safety webbing draped from the ceiling between blue lights. Fog used for fire drills on the ships pumped across the floor to hide the concrete beneath.

There was no bouncer at the door, but people were still hanging around the entrance.

As a rule, the fleet was cautious, and the young faces she saw belonged to fleet members who had never ventured outside their own crew more than a few times, even though the fleet had been grounded for nearly three years.

Tables to the left, bar ahead, dance floor to the right... and that meant the back half of the cargo hanger had been partitioned and karaoke would be in the back right corner. After a few minutes of weaving through the human crush, she found Gen, already sitting in Perrin Carver's lap and giggling.

"Selena!" Gen jumped up and hugged her. "I was beginning to worry!"

"How many people are in here?" Selena shouted over the music.

"Everyone under forty?" Gen laughed. With a small hand wave Gen put up a minor sound shield, muting the music. "People are going to stir crazy. Combine that with the anniversary—"

The anniversary.

Today.

The day the war had begun, the day the united fleet had died.

They'd been dying for four hundred

years, well aware that the reserve of orun crystals was depleted and there was no way to move forward with the ships they had.

Old Captain Baular had seen the deposit of orun on the fifth planet as their saving grace. He'd get it even if it meant killing the grounders.

And, coward that he was, he'd ordered his grandson to lead the first attack instead of leading it himself.

That opening skirmish began and ended in the dark, with Titan Sciarra in the infirmary, and five Academy fighters mis-sing or damaged. But by lunch of the next day, every officer belonging to crews allied with the Baulars withdrew.

Seven months later, heated words turned to live rounds.

"Selena?" Gen asked quietly, placing a hand on her arm. "You didn't know the date, did you?"

"I was trying not to think about." If she had, she'd have cut her vacation to the islands early. Maybe even made her pilgrimage to the small cay where she'd ditched her stolen fighter after driving off the attack.

She rolled her shoulder, stretching the deep scars. "It snuck up on me."

"First round, we drink to the Lost Fleet, and all who've gone on to crew it. I'm buying," Gen said with a touch of forced joviality. "Carver's been making friends. Tell her, babe." She pushed Carver's shoulder.

Perrin Carver was tall, broad-shouldered man with shy, hazel eyes that hid a wicked sense of humor.

Selena's heart fluttered just a little at the memory of a time when she'd fancied herself in love with him. He'd been the ideal starsider: intelligent, good-looking, and charismatic. They'd been friends of a sort, but even that relationship had soured when she'd realized he'd been getting close to her so he could learn more about Genevieve Silar.

Carver nodded and held out his hand. "Hi, Selena. How are you?"

She tapped the back of his hand with hers, letting him test her shields. "Good.

How's the Starguard?"

"Booming." The commander of the Starguard smiled, white teeth flashing, but there was a tightness around his eyes. "Everyone hears about guardians being allowed outside the Enclave, or working with the Jhandarmi, and I'm drowning in recruiting requests. Captains of larger crews invite me to Captain's Mess so they can introduce me to their best and brightest. Half the time I can't tell if they want me to marry into the crew or take the fleetlings into the guard." His shield was still attached to hers, scanning her as he talked.

All he would get from her was polite interest. Her heartrate didn't spike or dip at the mention of the Jhandarmi. Her smile never flickered.

"Maybe you should lock down Gen," Selena said. "If you had a spouse, no one would try to get you to marry into the crew."

Carver and Gen shared a look, and Gen sent a ping of information that Selena's implant translated as an ongoing debate over crew name and a place to live.

Carver sent something similar; a picture of his bachelor's quarters and his one ship.

There was no room for them to marry and have a family.

"Enclave is a temporary solution," Selena said out loud. She'd lost the taste for communicating by implant years ago. "If we—"

A heavy hand wrapped around her waist as someone wearing too much cologne stepped far too close to her. "Hello, Selena."

Hollis Silar, one of Gen's many siblings, kissed her temple.

Simultaneously, Selena sighed, sent a shock through her shield to Hollis's hand, and elbowed him in the gut. "Hi, Hollis. I see you're still bathing in cologne rather than water."

He stepped away from her, an easy smile still in place.

It wasn't that Hollis was bad looking; plenty of women found him handsome.

It was that he was equally affectionate

with every woman he saw and he couldn't keep a secret to save his life. Or anyone else's.

He'd chase anyone with a pretty smile and fell in and out of love a couple of times a day.

"Nice to see you too, Selena. Now, everyone, you're all going to look at me, smile, and laugh like I'm my normal, dashing self," he said, his smile never changing. "You haven't been paying attention, but I'm not a member of the Starguard for nothing. We're being watched. Now take your nice drinks from the waitress and keep your eyes on me."

Hollis nodded to the waitress and handed out four cups with bright purple liquid. "Bruised Stars all around. Guaranteed to make you giggle, or so the guy at the bar told me. Although he's a Seutaai, so take it with a shield in place." He handed Selena her drink with a smile, but turned immediately to glance over his shoulder.

"Big brother, who are we looking for?" Gen asked with a slow drawl. "Is it a friend who you might have forgotten to call back after a night out?"

Hollis shook his head. "No, I thought I saw some of the Lee crew. Make that, I'm certain of it."

Selena grimaced. "As long as Rowena isn't here."

"Did you call me?"

Startled, Selena looked up to the face of her least favorite woman: Rowena Lee.

"Hello," Selena said politely. "I see you're still alive. That's..."

Unfortunate.

She nodded and took a slug of her Bruised Star.

Rowena held up a tray of electric blue shots. "My crew thinks I can't out-drink anyone in this bar. I probably can't go toe-to-toe with alcoholics like the Silars here. But No-Shot Selena?" Rowena set the drinks on the table. "I can out-shoot you in the stars or on the ground."

Gen sucked in air between her teeth and sent Selena several urgent pings telling her to ignore the Lees.

Selena muted Gen. "I took plenty of

shots in the war. As I recall, I disabled three of your big birds. *Bassi*, *Aryton*, *Theoano*… Bang, bang, bang." Selena mimed firing with her finger. "Three shots. Three silent ships."

"Not kills," Rowena said. "A whole war and you never blooded yourself."

That was it, the memory she didn't want to face; the time she'd almost taken Death's claim and risked killing someone outside of war.

"That's uncalled for," Hollis said, trying to step between them. "Selena, why don't we—"

Selena pushed Hollis aside and grabbed the first shot.

She tossed back the potent drink and shattered the glass on the table. "Go suck vacuum, Rowena. You're a pissant yeoman with no hope of command."

"I went to the Academy, same as you, Selena. I fought for the fleet." Rowena slammed a shot back. "You fought for the mud-lickers."

Selena took another shot as the first started to fuzz her judgement. "I prevented the Baulars from committing mass genocide and destroying the civilians along with the fleet."

Rowena took her second shot. A crowd was gathering and that seemed to feed her cruelty. "The Lees survived the war. We're still here. How many Caryll captains are there? Oh, right, one. Can you count that high, No-Shot? You have any idea how easy it would be for me to end you right now?"

Selena took the last two glasses and slammed them both back.

Gen pinged her, giving locations, counts, and identities of the Lee allies in the crowd.

Hollis stepped to her flank, ready to defend her.

She stood, anger burning through her veins. "Sure, your crew outnumbers mine. I guess on paper, it's not really a fair fight, is it, Rowena? But you were trained as a flight leader, and what do Carylls do? Hand-to-hand combat. Maybe I should thin your ranks, starting with one mouthy yeoman."

Keep reading! Head to:
www.inkprintpress.com/sfrom/malik/bodies/

ABOUT THE AUTHOR

LIANA BROOKS is not a spy, an officer with any intelligence force, or an assassin, but she likes to write about them all the same.

When she isn't swimming, she enjoys writing science fiction in every form, from sprawling space operas (*Fleet of Malik*) to the antics of a superhero family (*Heroes and Villains*).

You can learn more about her and her books at www.LianaBrooks.com.

INKLETS

Collect them all! Released on the 1st and 15th of each month.

INKLET #031
Welcome to Dark Dale
LIANA BROOKS

INKLET #030
When War Came to Town
A Powers Story
AMY LAURENS

INKLET #032
Not Fantasy
AMY LAURENS

INKLET #034
Courting the Winter Prince
LIANA BROOKS

INKLET #035
At the Home of the Winter King
A Powers Story
AMY LAURENS

INKLET #036
With This Ring
AMY LAURENS

INKLET #037
Venus &
Seven Reasons I Said No
LIANA BROOKS

INKLET #038
OATH KEEPER
AMY LAURENS

INKLET #039
FORGET
A Powers Story
AMY LAURENS

Not Quite Cinderella
LIANA BROOKS

ONE BAD MAN
AMY LAURENS

DOUBLE ISSUE
The Claustrophobia Of Loneliness &
Adam, Be A Star
AMY LAURENS

The Artist as a Young Girl
LIANA BROOKS

CONFESSIONS
AMY LAURENS

But For Snow
A Kaditeos Story
AMY LAURENS

The Boy Named NO
LIANA BROOKS

Anamata
AMY LAURENS

A Wolf for Christmas
AMY LAURENS